Abuelita's Secret Matzahs

Written by
Sandy Eisenberg Sasso

Illustrations by
Diana Bryer

emmis
books

For further information, contact the publisher at

Emmis Books
1700 Madison Road
Cincinnati, OH 45206
www.emmisbooks.com

ISBN 1-57860-157-6

Library of Congress Control Number: 2004117550

Cover and interior designed by Andrea Kupper
Edited by Jessica Yerega

Dedication

To Dennis, "mi querido," who opened windows to the Sephardic heritage. S.E.S.

To Isabelle Medina Sandoval, who continues to inspire me about all things Jewish. D.B.

Acknowledgments

My gratitude to Dr. Stanley Hordes, Adjunct Research Professor at the Latin American and Iberian Institute, University of New Mexico, for his careful reading of the manuscript and expert advice. A special thanks to Claudette Einhorn for Jacobo's favorite recipe. S.E.S.

Jacobo loved to visit his grandmother, especially on Easter. She lived in Santa Fe, New Mexico. Her *adobe* house was hidden by juniper and piñon trees and sat under the shade of the cottonwood.

Jacobo loved the red and purple mountains that looked like someone had painted them onto the sky. He loved his grandmother's *pastelitos*, sweet flan, and *sopa*—bread pudding with raisins she always made for a special treat.

Easter was a special time. *Abuelita,* as Jacobo called his grandmother, would help him paint Easter eggs the color of the mountains and the sun. On Easter morning Jacobo would get up early to hunt for the eggs his grandmother had hidden among the bushes and trees in her yard. Then they would eat a quick breakfast of warm tortillas, cheese, and milk before going to church.

Jacobo liked the church, which was of brown adobe like Abuelita's house. He liked to hear the priest mix Spanish and English in the prayers, and he loved the songs.

Easter was different in his grandmother's house. During *Semana Santa,* Holy Week, they would eat *torta de huevo* and lentil soup with onion like all his friends. But on Easter, his friends would serve ham and biscuits with sweet butter. But not at his grandmother's house. They never ate *carne de cerdo,* pork. And during Semana Santa his grandmother never ate bread or his favorite *sopaipillas* with honey. She only served tortillas made without any yeast.

"Abuelita," Jacobo asked, "why don't we eat pork like my friends?"

"Ah, *mijito,* my child," she answered, "it is the way of our family."

That was the answer that Abuelita always gave. When he asked her why they did not eat bread and butter or sopaipillas with honey during Holy Week, she smiled and said, "It is the way of our family."

"But why is it the way of our family?" Jacobo insisted on knowing.

"Mijito, you ask too many questions."

One Easter a new family moved next door to Abuelita. One of the children was Jacobo's age. His name was David. Jacobo and David became close friends.

Jacobo learned that David's family didn't eat pork. When he asked David why, David told him that it was because they were Jewish.

When Jacobo told his grandmother that David didn't eat pork because he was Jewish, she simply sighed and said, "That's nice, mijito. I am glad that you are friends."

One day Jacobo noticed a candelabrum sitting on a shelf in David's house. "Wow, David, you know that my grandmother has a candelabrum just like yours, and we always light it on Christmas."

"On Christmas?" David was puzzled. "Our candelabrum is called a *menorah,* and we light it on the holiday of Hanukkah."

When Jacobo told his grandmother that David's candelabrum was called a menorah, she pretended that she didn't hear him.

When Jacobo had dinner at David's house on Friday nights, David's mother always lit two candles and said a blessing over them. Jacobo knew that his grandmother lit two candles in her room every Friday night. She would close all the curtains, put her shawl over her head, and whisper something so that no one could hear. Jacobo decided that there was no use in asking why on Friday evenings his grandmother lit two candles just like David's mom. He would just get the same answer: "It's the way of our family."

That year David invited Jacobo to join his family for the Passover *Seder*. Jacobo had never been to a Seder before. He loved listening to the story of how the people of Israel escaped the Pharaoh who had made them slaves and how the Israelites crossed the sea to freedom. He liked the dipping of parsley into salt water to remember the tears of the slaves. Most of all he liked listening to David ask the four questions. He, too, wanted to know why on all other nights they ate all kinds of bread, but on this night of Passover, only unleavened bread. Maybe it was the same reason his grandmother did not eat bread, but only flat tortillas during Semana Santa.

Jacobo learned that the unleavened bread they ate at the Seder was called *matzah*. David told him that they ate matzah during Passover because the Israelites were in such a hurry to leave Egypt that they had no time to let their bread rise. Matzah was a reminder of the hard life of slaves. It was the bread the Israelites carried with them to freedom.

Jacobo was amazed. "You know that at my grandmother's we eat only unleavened bread during Easter. My grandmother's tortillas are Easter matzahs!"

Everyone at the Seder table smiled. No one in David's family had ever heard of Easter matzahs.

The next day when Jacobo went to church for Easter Mass, he asked the priest if he had ever heard of Easter matzahs. He never had.

That night Jacobo had more than four questions to ask his grandmother. "Abuelita, David's family has a candelabrum just like yours. David's family never eats pork, and neither do we. David's mom lights two candles on Friday nights, just like you. And David's family eats matzahs during Passover, just like we eat tortillas during Holy Week. No one has ever heard of Easter matzahs. Everyone in the church eats ham and bacon. No one in the church eats tortillas for Holy Week. No one has a candelabrum like David's and ours. Please tell me, Abuelita, why is this the way of our family?"

"Come, mijito," said Jacobo's grandmother, "Sit with me on the porch. It is time to tell you the secret of our family. A very long time ago your ancestors lived in Spain. They were *judíos*, Jews. For many centuries they lived freely and practiced their religion without fear. Then a queen named Isabella and a king named Ferdinand became rulers of all of Spain. They and their advisors decided that Jews could stay in Spain only if they became Catholic. They wanted one law, one religion for everybody.

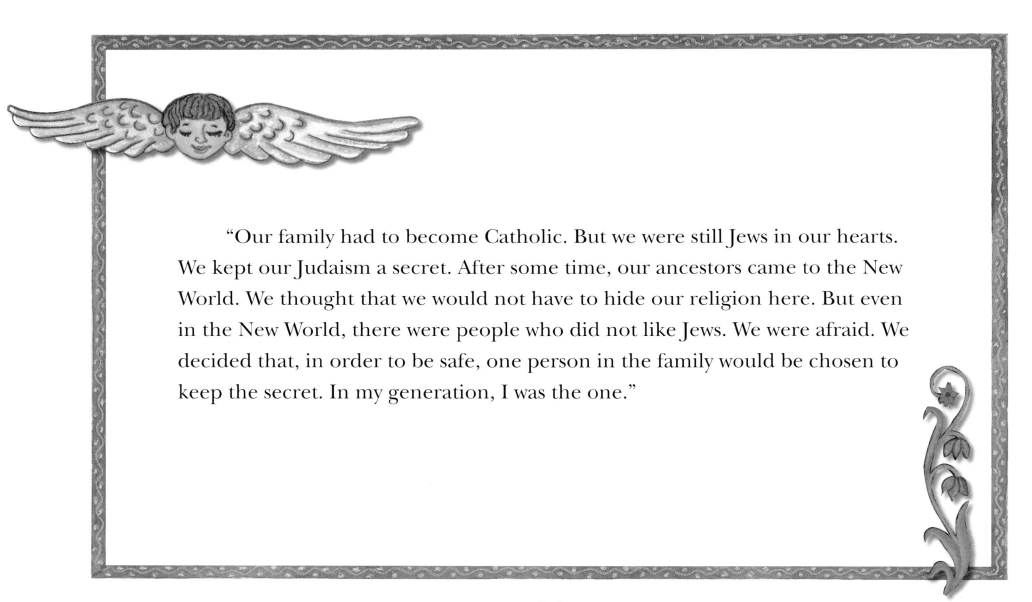

"Our family had to become Catholic. But we were still Jews in our hearts. We kept our Judaism a secret. After some time, our ancestors came to the New World. We thought that we would not have to hide our religion here. But even in the New World, there were people who did not like Jews. We were afraid. We decided that, in order to be safe, one person in the family would be chosen to keep the secret. In my generation, I was the one."

His grandmother reached into her pocket and took out an old iron key. "Jacobo, this is the key that unlocked the door of our family's home in Spain. Whoever was told the secret was given this key. Now it is yours. You will be the one in your generation to hold the key and know the secret."

Jacobo could not believe what he was hearing. He put his hands over his ears. He did not want to know this secret. He went to Mass. He was studying for Confirmation with the priest. He celebrated Christmas and Easter. He was glad that David and his family did not have to hide the fact that they were Jews. But he never thought of himself as a Jew.

Jacobo stood up, folded his arms across his chest, and shouted, "Why didn't you tell me before? I always asked you questions. You never answered me!"

Jacobo looked at his grandmother and could see tears in her eyes. He knelt down and put her hand in his. "What am I to do with this key?" he asked softly. "Who am I, Abuelita? Am I a Catholic or a Jew?"

"As you grow up, mijito, that will be for you to decide." His grandmother wrapped him in her arms and held him close for a long time.

Jacobo took the key and placed it in his shirt pocket, close to his heart.

GLOSSARY

adobe	brick baked in the sun
pastelitos	small pastry filled with fruit or meat
flan	custard
sopa	usually soup, used by some New Mexicans as name for special bread pudding
tortillas	flat unleavened flour or corn bread
Semana Santa	Holy Week
torta de huevo	egg omelet
carne de cerdo	pork
sopaipillas	bread fritters that are dipped in honey
abuelita	endearing term for grandmother
mijito	abbreviation for "mi hijito," an endearing term for "my child"
menorah	a lamp, candelabrum used for Hanukkah
Seder	the Passover meal
matzah	unleavened bread used on Passover
Passover	the Jewish holiday of freedom celebrating the Israelites' Exodus from Egypt
judíos	Jews

Jacobo's Favorite Sopa

1 ½ cups water

2 teaspoons cinnamon

1 cup brown sugar

3 ½ cups toasted raisin bread that has been buttered and cut into small pieces

2 cups grated longhorn or Monterey jack cheese

1 cup raisins

Place layer of bread in 8-by-8-inch square pan. Add raisins and cheese alternately until all ingredients are used. Dissolve brown sugar and cinnamon in water. Pour over bread mixture and bake in oven at 350° for 30 minutes or until all liquid is absorbed. Serve hot or cold.